Sto   ur

2/95

ALLEN COUNTY PUBLIC LIBRARY

FORT WAYNE, INDIANA 46802

You may return this book to any location of

the Allen County Public Library.

DEMCO

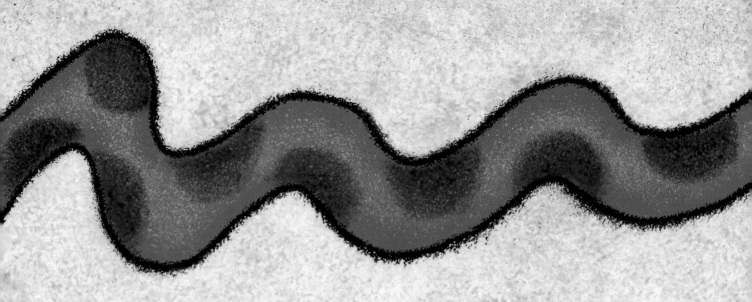

A Most Unusual Lunch

Robert Bender

Dial Books for Young Readers
New York

Published by Dial Books for Young Readers
A Division of Penguin Books USA Inc.
375 Hudson Street
New York, New York 10014

Designed by Julie Rauer
Printed in Hong Kong

First Edition
1 3 5 7 9 10 8 6 4 2

Library of Congress Cataloging in Publication Data
Bender, Robert.
A most unusual lunch / Robert Bender.
p.   cm.
Summary: A frog is strangely transformed after
eating a beetle, as is the fish who devours the frog, and
so on, in this humorous cumulative story.
ISBN 0-8037-1710-5 (trade).—ISBN 0-8037-1711-3 (library)
[1. Food chains (Ecology)—Fiction.
2. Animals—Fiction.]   I. Title.
PZ7.B43147Mo 1994 [E]—dc20 93-34068 CIP AC

The full-color art was produced with animator's paint on
acetate that is then backed with black paper.
This provides the dark outlines around the images.

Dedicated to Debora,
my adopted grandmother

One day a frog swallowed a beetle whole because he was hungry.

The next day the frog woke up with two antennae on his head, plus six tiny little legs on his underbelly.

When he leaned over the edge of his lily pad to splash
some cold water on his face...

a big fish rushed over and gulped him down.

Later when the fish looked in his underwater mirror, he saw that he had grown two antennae, six tiny little legs on his underbelly, AND two big green legs.

So he hopped out of the pond to test his new parts.

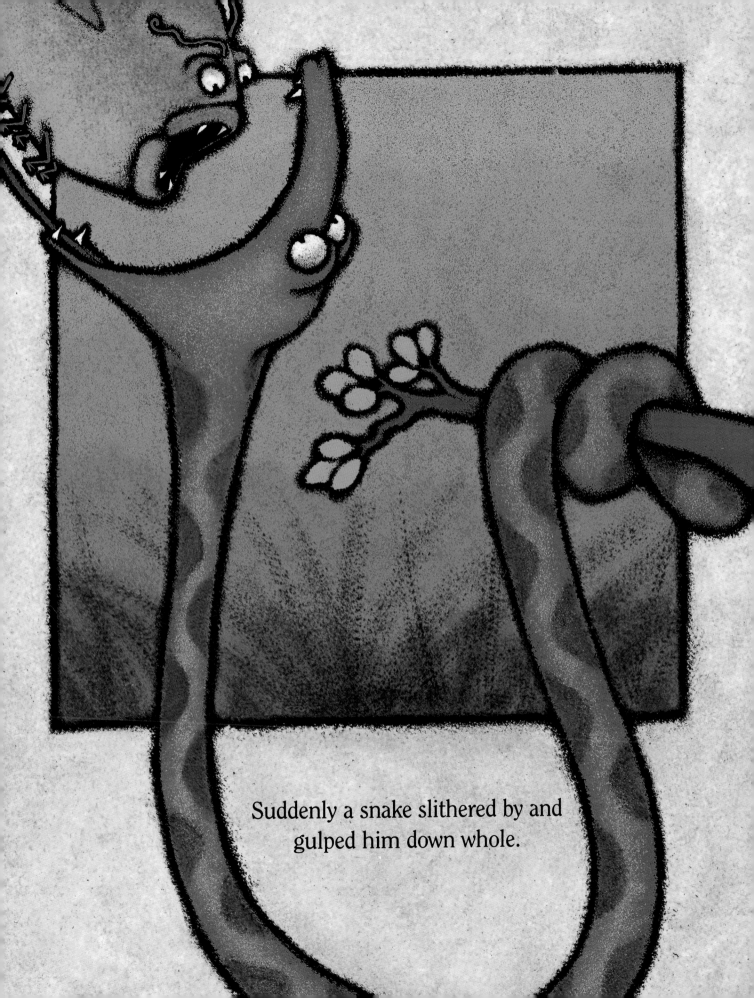

Suddenly a snake slithered by and
gulped him down whole.

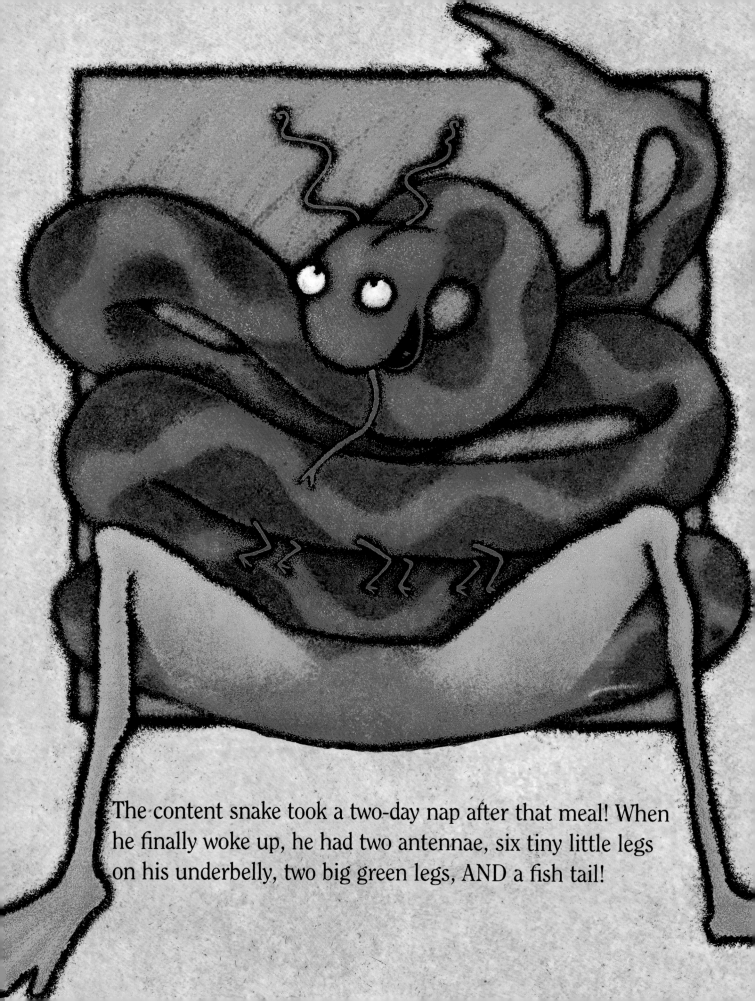

The content snake took a two-day nap after that meal! When he finally woke up, he had two antennae, six tiny little legs on his underbelly, two big green legs, AND a fish tail!

He thought that this was very interesting. He crawled on his six new tiny little legs, hopped around on his big green legs, and swatted at the flies with his new fish tail. He was having such a good time that he didn't notice when he crawled right into the mouth of...

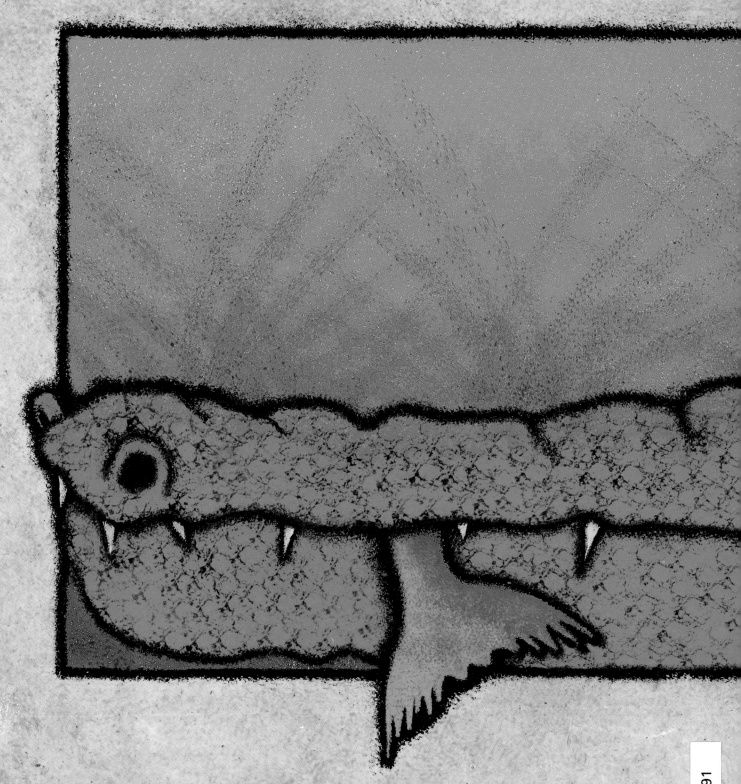

a waiting crocodile. The crocodile was so hungry that he
swallowed the whole snake with one snap of his jaws! He was
pleased with his lunch, and went to take a nap in the sun while
he digested his food.

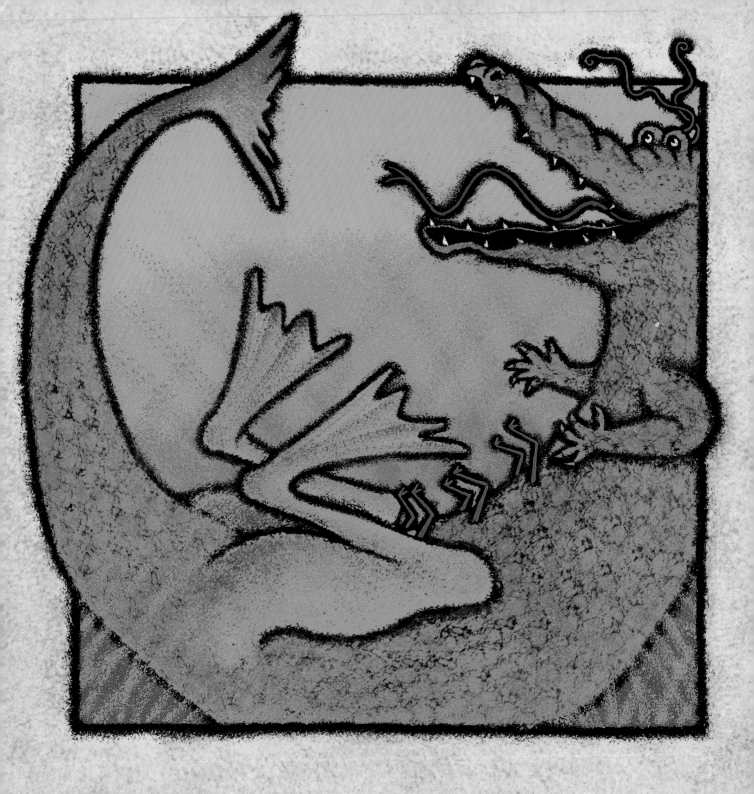

When the crocodile awoke and yawned, a long forked tongue popped out of his mouth. Not only that, he also had two antennae, six tiny little legs on his underbelly, two big green legs, AND a fish tail that rattled!

A nearby lion heard the rattling and came running. He was so hungry that he opened his mouth as wide as he could and swallowed the crocodile in one gulp!

Of course, when the lion awoke from his nap, he had two antennae, six tiny little legs on his underbelly, two big green legs, a fish tail that rattled, a long forked tongue, PLUS strange scales all over his body!

Well, the lion was not very pleased with these changes. After all, the lion is the king of the jungle, and kings are perfect just as they are.

So he gave out a great belch!

Out popped the crocodile who had two antennae, six tiny little legs on his underbelly, two big green legs, a fish tail that rattled, and a long forked tongue.

The crocodile was very happy to get out of the lion's uncomfortable stomach. When he opened his mouth to thank the lion...

out popped the snake—with two antennae, six tiny little legs on his underbelly, two big green legs, and a fish tail.

The snake in turn was pleasantly surprised to see the light of day. He opened his mouth to test his forked tongue, and out popped the fish who had two antennae, six tiny little legs on his underbelly, and two big green legs.

The fish splashed into a nearby pond and opened his mouth to
release a couple of bubbles. When he did, the frog with two
antennae and six tiny little legs leaped out.

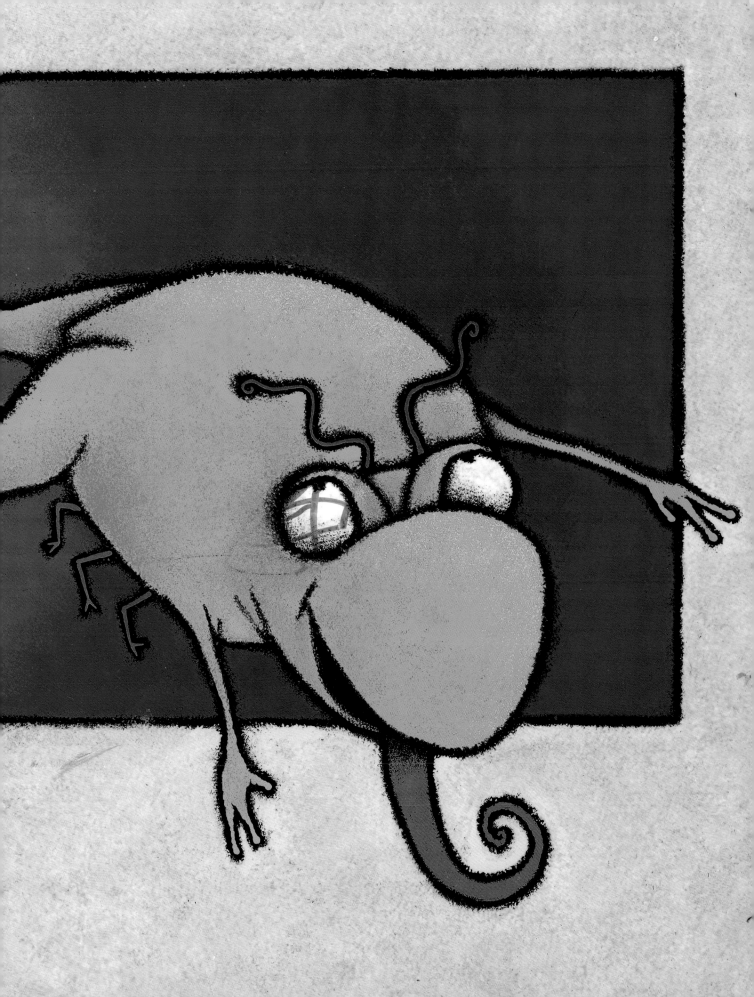

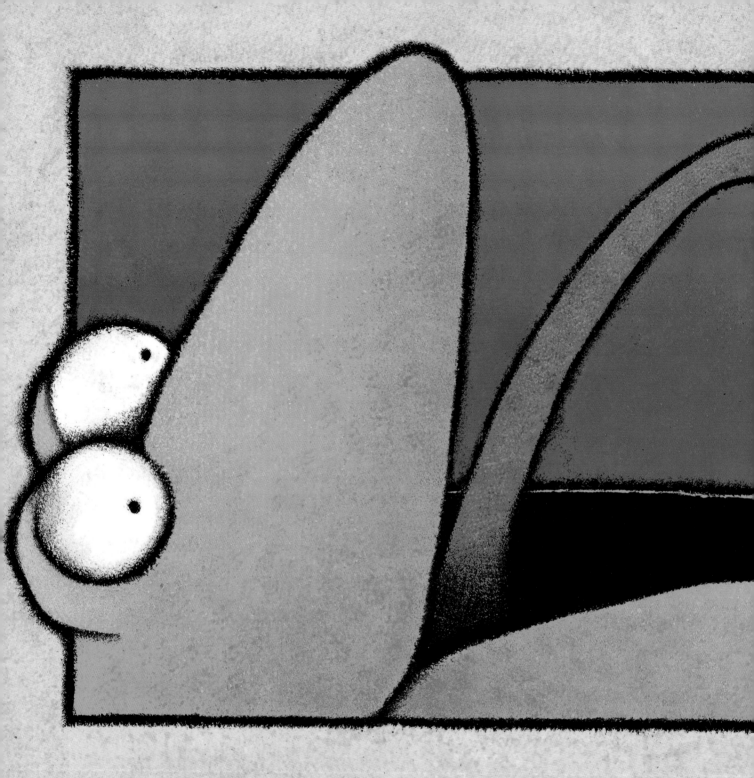

The frog immediately rejoiced by exclaiming "Ribbit" to anyone who could hear.

That is when the little beetle who had just his own two antennae and six tiny little legs popped out.

Then the little beetle joined the frog, the big fish, the slithering snake, the hungry crocodile, and the lion, in a big celebration

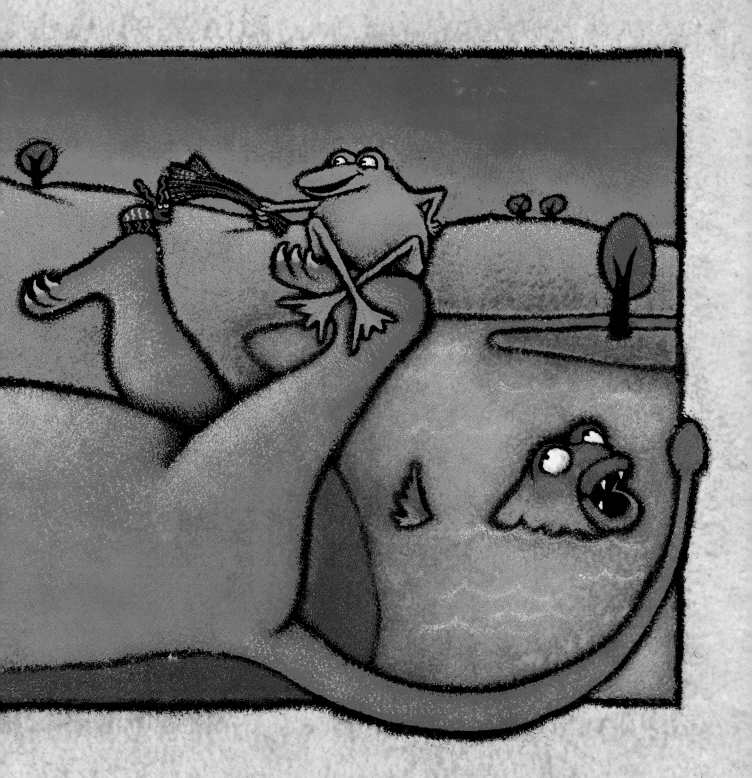

where they tried to satisfy their hunger by eating lots of grass
and leaves. Until…

the frog thought he might like dessert!

The End?